S0-DVF-797

KATIE'S
•HAND-ME-DOWN DAY•

Story by Laurie Wark • Art by Eugenie Fernandes

Kids Can Press Ltd., Toronto

Kids Can Press Ltd. acknowledges with appreciation the assistance of the Canada Council and the Ontario Arts Council in the production of this book.

Canadian Cataloguing in Publication Data

Wark, Laurie
Katie's hand-me-down day

ISBN 1-55074-159-4

I. Fernandes, Eugenie, 1943– II. Title.

PS8595.A75K3 1994 jC813'.54 C94-930762-9
PZ7.W37Ka 1994

The art in this book was rendered in gouache, oil pastels and water-colour pencils on Arches water-colour paper.

Kids Can Press Ltd.
29 Birch Avenue
Toronto, Ontario, Canada
M4V 1E2

Edited by Debbie Rogosin
Designed by N.R.Jackson
Cover design by Karen Powers
Printed in Hong Kong by Wing King Tong Company Limited

94 0 9 8 7 6 5 4 3

In memory of Joe Wark, who handed down so much
L.W.

For Barbara
E.F.

On the day before she turned five years old, Katie decided that she was too grown-up to be the hand-me-down kid any more.

She had hand-me-down boots from her brother Benjamin, a hand-me-down sweater from her sister Susan, hand-me-down jeans passed on to Susan by their cousin Janine, and even a hand-me-down raincoat given to Benjamin by the nephew of the lady across the way.

These weren't just hand-me-downs. By the time they were passed on to Katie, they were hand-me-down-down-downs.

As far as Katie could tell, she'd never had anything firsthand, never-been-used, brand-spanking-new.

And that's exactly what she wanted for her birthday — something new of her very own. So today, Katie and Dad were going shopping.

Katie wanted her very own, firsthand, never-been-used, brand-spanking-new pair of boots. They would be bright and shiny and have that funny new smell, and she would be the first one to wear them to jump and splash in muddy puddles.

At the store, Katie headed for the shoe department. She was amazed. There were so many different kinds of boots. Katie looked at them all and tried on most of them. She was having a difficult time making up her mind.

"Gosh," said Dad. "I remember when Benjamin used to wear those boots to the pond."

"He wore those boots to the pond?" Katie asked.

"He'd spend hours there skipping stones," answered Dad.

"I bet *I* could learn how to skip stones," said Katie.

"You know, now that you're old enough, maybe Benjamin will teach you," said Dad. "Too bad you won't have the old boots for luck."

Katie pulled on one of the old boots and looked in the mirror. She decided that there were just too many boots to choose from. Besides, Benjamin's boots weren't that bad, and maybe they *would* bring her luck.

What I need, thought Katie, is my very own, firsthand, never-been-used, brand-spanking-new sweater. I'll choose the colour myself, and someday I'll hand it down to someone else. Katie headed for the sweater department.

Since red was her favourite colour, Katie decided that she would only try on sweaters with red in them.

"I remember when Grandma knit this sweater a long time ago," said Dad dreamily.

"Grandma made that sweater?" asked Katie, and she took a closer look. "Maybe she could show me how to knit."

Katie wanted to knit a long red scarf for Dad, just like the scarves Grandma knit.

"I'll bet you're old enough to learn," said Dad. "Grandma could teach you this summer when she comes to visit."

Katie was tired of trying on sweaters — there were so many, and they all made her hot and itchy. She looked again at the sweater that Grandma had knit. She really liked that old sweater — it wasn't hot or itchy, and it *did* have red in it.

Katie looked down at the patch on her jeans.

"That's it! I'll have my very own, firsthand, never-been-used, brand-spanking-new pair of jeans," declared Katie. "And I'll choose my very own patches."

Katie headed for the jeans department.

When she tried the jeans on, Katie was too small for some and too big for others.

Dad chuckled. “I remember when Susan got the rip in those jeans. She was learning to ride her two-wheeler.”

Katie glanced at the patch as she tried to button a pair of too-small jeans.

“I'm big enough to ride a two-wheeler now,” said Katie. “Maybe Susan will let me try her bike.”

Dad smiled. He suggested that Katie get a big pair of jeans, so she could grow into them, but Katie wanted a pair that fit as well as the old jeans.

Just then, Katie spotted some bright new raincoats with ducks on them. That's it, she thought. I need my very own, firsthand, never-been-used, brand-spanking-new raincoat. Katie headed for the coats.

She loved the ducks. They were perfect. Just as she was trying to decide between the yellow ducks and the blue ducks, Dad gave a big sigh. Katie sighed, too.

Dad said wistfully, “Susan used to wear this raincoat when she filled the birdbaths, and Benjamin wore it before her.”

“I'd like to fill the birdbaths,” said Katie.

“Well,” said Dad, “now that you're old enough, I think that job can be handed down to you.”

Katie couldn't believe her ears. She loved to watch the birds. The cardinals were her favourite. She couldn't wait to get home and check the birdbaths.

Dad liked the yellow ducks, but Katie was pulling on her old raincoat. She had made up her mind.

She thought that, for now, she would keep the lucky hand-me-down boots from her brother Benjamin, the cosy hand-me-down sweater from her sister Susan, the comfy hand-me-down jeans from her cousin Janine, and even the hand-me-down raincoat from the nephew of the lady across the way.

Katie decided that what she really wanted was a strawberry sundae.

So Dad and Katie shared the biggest sundae Katie had ever seen, and then they went home.

Later that day, Katie wore her boots to the pond with Benjamin and learned to skip stones. She called Grandma to ask her about knitting, and she filled up the birdbaths.

She even tried Susan's two-wheeler. She fell a few times, but now there was a hole in her jeans for her very own patch.

That night, as Katie pulled on her special handmade sweater over her pyjamas, she decided that it wasn't so bad being the hand-me-down kid after all.

As she drifted off to sleep, Katie didn't hear Dad wheel the firsthand, never-been-used, brand-spanking-new, bright red bicycle into her room for her birthday surprise in the morning.